Guy in the Afterlife

A Story from a Dog's Perspective

Patricia E. Flinn

Also by Eugene C. Flinn and Patricia E. Flinn

Fiction

Guy, the Dog Who Loved Books

The Spring Lake Murders

Murder at SeaScapes Village

A Different Kind of Love Story

Bathtub Magic in Cherry Blossom Village

Boyd to Malachy to Chance

Penfield Prep, Volume One; Penfield Prep, Volume Two

The Inn of the Seventy-Seven Clocks

Skytrain Over Lake Winnipesaukee

Trapped in the English Department

The Counterfeit Nun

Alibi for Murder

The Mystery on Logan Lane

The 1774 House

Rimsky

The Love Château

From Flaubert with Love

The Listerine Lunatic Hits Hoboken and Other Strange Tales

It Happened in Hoboken: Comic Tale from the Waterfront City

One More for the Road: 40 Tales from Hoboken, & Ireland

The Accidental Tea Room

The Castle Murders

The Metamorphosis of a Hedge Fund Manager

Non-Fiction

The Literary Guide to the United States
Telling the School Story

Children's Story

Trixie Triphammer's Magical Christmas

Copyright © 2017 Patricia E. Flinn
All rights reserved.

Special thanks to Claire McLeod, editor

ISBN-13: 9781545445464
ISBN-10: 154544546X
Library of Congress Control Number: 2017906216
CreateSpace Independent Publishing Platform
North Charleston, South Carolina

For Precocious Children Everywhere

To love another person is to see the face of God

Victor Hugo
Les Miserables, 1862

For Gene and Guy:

Best Buddies Forever

You're Here, There, and Everywhere

For Guy, Our Golden Retriever

Your jaws gobbled food
Like a garbage compressor;
You usually fell asleep
Where rooms narrowed into doors;
When I was in my bare feet
You always stepped on my toes.

And now, my dear friend,
You have left us,
Flying from our lives
As graceful as a sea bird.
In your last sad days with us
You displayed a quiet courage,
Bearing the pain,
Sensing the change ahead,
And returning our last greetings
With a cheerful wag
Of your tail.

As you lay dying, Guy,
I saw all of us in you:
A run, a dash, a bite of food,
And a sudden end to it all
That is not really as gradual
As they say it is,
For the expected
Is never really expected
Or satisfactorily explained.

E.C. Flinn

Guy

If you should ever stumble on
A doggie named Guy de Maupassant
Then watch your wallet, and watch your keys
For Guy eats everything he sees.

Guy, Guy, Guy de Maupassant
Full of mischief, day and night
He'll grab your shoelaces, hanky too
And retrieve everything in sight.

On Christmas Eve I spotted Guy
A-hiding behind the Christmas tree
Determined Santa should not pass
Until Guy bit him in the ass.

E.C.. Flinn

They are not dead who live in the hearts
they leave behind.

Tuscarora

What is life? It is the flash of a firefly in
the night. It is the breath of a buffalo in the winter-
time. It is the little shadow which runs across the grass
and loses itself in the sunset.

Blackfoot

When Laura Finneran came home from school one afternoon in early March, she learned from her mother that Guy, their lovely golden retriever, had died that morning.

Laura was distraught over the sad and unexpected news and she cried so hard her mother thought she would float away on her tears and vanish into a pool of sadness.

"Guy is now in doggie heaven," Laura's mother said, hugging her daughter as she wiped away her tears. "He is much happier now since he is not sick anymore."

Laura knew Guy had been getting older and no longer had the energy of a young dog, and she realized he had trouble getting up from the floor and walking about, but she never imagined that he would die from these things.

"He died because his heart gave out," Laura's mother explained. "We just didn't realize how sick he really was."

It was hard to imagine Guy's heart giving out since he was always so loving and brave. Despite the severe weakness in his legs and the pain he might have been feeling, Guy always managed to do his business in the back yard, never once soiling the house or himself. Every night, no matter how exhausted he was, he wagged his tail and followed Laura into the bedroom where he slept protectively beside her.

When Laura remembered all these things about her beloved friend and how handsome and gentle he was, her heart ached with longing.

"You must think about all the good things when you think about Guy," she said, trying her best to comfort her. "Guy died peacefully, and now he's a young healthy dog again in heaven watching down on us with lots of love.

Laura, who always asked questions about subjects that seemed to have no answers, was not at all reassured by her mother's words.

Although she wanted to believe that her beloved Guy was still somewhere, she had no way of really knowing if that were true. All she knew was that Guy was no longer there waiting for her in the kitchen when she arrived home with her school books and trusty backpack.

She wanted Guy back again, doing what he always did—smiling and springing up from his bed when he heard her entering the front door and rushing over to her with his tail wagging and his big fluffy body swaying from left to right.

Now Guy's bed was empty, and he was not sitting attentively waiting for the cookie or peanut butter sandwich left over from lunch. He was nowhere in the house or backyard. As far as she was concerned, he was just gone forever.

Laura cried and cried, her heart cleaving over the loss of her best friend whom she had grown up with.

When Laura's father arrived home later that evening, he tried to comfort her, but since he also missed Guy and was very sad too, he was not much help.

That night Laura went to bed very early, skipping dinner, television, and even her homework which she did faithfully every night. Under the covers in her dark bedroom where Guy used to sleep beside her, Laura lay awake and thought for hours.

She couldn't imagine what it was like to die. Did Guy fly up into space like a cloud of smoke from a wood fire that had just gone out? Or did his spirit rise up slowly from his body and leave it behind the way a person would lift herself from a warm bed to greet a new day? Was Guy afraid when all this was happening to him? Whenever something new and strange happened to Laura, she was always afraid.

She remembered when it was time to leave third grade and enter fourth with a brand new teacher and some new friends. She didn't know what to expect and so she imagined the worst. She would be alone. No one would like her. The teacher would be unkind and very demanding. Laura saw herself failing every subject and having to attend summer school while all her classmates went on vacation and laughed at her. Her mother and father tried to reassure her that all would be well after a day or two, but the only one who brought Laura comfort was Guy who would curl up on her lap, wagging his tail and licking away her tears. But just as her parents had predicted, after a few days Laura liked fourth grade a lot and didn't miss or think too much about what she left behind.

She wondered if Guy would feel the same way about his new life. Would he miss her and his days on earth as part of a loving family? Or would he be happy in his new home running through wide open fields after tennis balls and Frisbees the way he once did? Would there be other dogs to play with and lots of good food to eat whenever he got tired and hungry?

All these questions haunted Laura as she lay in her dark bedroom and thought about Guy. She longed to see and talk with him again. Maybe he would tell her many secrets about what it was like to die and enter a strange new place.

Laura wondered about all these things long into the night even though she had to get up early in the morning to go to school. When her parents came into her room to say good night, she pretended to be asleep, so she wouldn't upset them with her tears.

Sometime after midnight when the sky above her house ceased weeping stars, Laura closed her eyes and fell into a very deep sleep.

Soft and enticing crystal moonlight spilled from a nearby window and bathed the room with a magical translucent charm. It invited her to follow its intoxicating spell into the night sky. She floated off the bed and drifted upward like a delicate leaf carried along by a warm breeze.

Rays of light were dancing all around her and everything she looked at seemed to shimmer and pulse with vibrating energy.

"Laura," a voice echoed within the chambers of her mind, "Isn't this amazing? You thought about me and here we are together again."

"Guy? Is that you?"

Guy: A handsome and gentle dog

"Yes, Laura, it's me. I know it's strange, but in this new state so different from the earth, we can talk together just by opening our minds to thoughts that we want to communicate."

"But where are you? I can't see you."

"I'm what people call a spirit now and not everyone can see spirits, but if you wish and imagine hard enough, you will soon be able to see me and other spirits too."

"Oh, I wish that very much," Laura said. "I love you and I want more than anything to see you again."

Suddenly the powerful energy that was vibrating everywhere, passed directly through her, and then grew brighter with an intense rainbow of color that spun into many radiant shapes sending off burning sparks of starlight that coalesced into the body of a beautiful golden retriever.

"Guy," Laura cried excitedly. "I can see you now."

"You took a short cut to seeing," Guy said, leaping into her arms and licking her face with joy. "Once you said the magic word *love* your eyes opened, and you were able to see."

"Oh, you look and feel so good," Laura said, hugging him tightly. "You're like a young dog again, and I'm so glad you're not sick anymore."

"Sickness is something that happens only on earth," Guy explained. "There is no sickness here."

Growing up together

"Are we in heaven then?"

"You can call it that if you want to, but everyone has a different opinion and name for it."

"Do you like it here?'

"Oh, yes. I love it here. I get to do so many things I could never do on earth."

"Like what?"

"I can fly, I can pass through walls, and I can see and hear things that are happening very far away. Best of all, I never get sleepy because I have no body and there is no time."

"No time?"

The earth is blue

"Nope. I know that is hard to understand since on earth everyone is always looking at clocks and watches, but here time doesn't exist. Past, present and future are all connected like a long train on an imaginary track going everywhere at once."

"Wow, that sounds cool," Laura gasped. "I would like to take a ride on that kind of train any day."

"It's hard getting used to at first, but once you understand how it works, you never want to go back to the old way of thinking again."

"It's amazing how fast you've learned to talk, Guy. You sound so smart now. On earth you never said anything and the only words you understood really well were *cookie, walk, dinner, play, Frisbee, and eat*."

"Leaving the earth behind or the *obstructed universe* as I like to call it, opens up a lot of new doors and windows," Guy teased. "On earth everything, --dogs, cats, mice, elephants, people-- all have bodies and because of that they are limited in many ways. Now don't get me wrong, Laura. Bodies are great when you need them, and I really enjoyed mine for years until I got old and sick, but once you enter the *Afterlife*, as I like to call it, everything changes. You're not limited anymore by a three-dimensional body."

"Am I in the *Afterlife* now?" Laura asked, looking around her.

"Yes, you are. That's why we can talk like this."

The wonder of the universe

"But I haven't died. I just went to sleep as usual."

"That's right. Some people can come here without dying and learn lots of things. You did that Laura, when you desired so strongly to see me again. You left your body only temporarily to visit with me."

"But if I like it here can I stay?"

"Mommy and Daddy would be very upset if you don't go back to them, Laura, just as you were upset when you believed I was gone forever."

Vibrating energy everywhere

"I never want to upset them. I love them just as much as I love you."

"I know. That's why you should go back soon."

"But I want to be with you too."

"And you always will be. All you have to do is think of me, and I'll be right there with you."

"Really? It's that simple?"

"Cross my heart and hope *to die*," Guy laughed, sending sparks of humor everywhere. "That's how things work here."

"That's great."

"On earth most people believe only what their bodies tell them is real. They see themselves as separate from everything else, and that makes them feel sad and alone."

"That how I felt when I thought I'd never see you again."

"I know, Laura, and that's how I felt too until I got here and realized there is no such thing as separation. That's only something people on earth believe."

"Like Time?"

"Yes. Here everyone knows everything is connected and continually moving and flowing like individual waves surfacing for a moment in the vast ocean."

"Speaking of the ocean, I remember how you loved swimming there when we took you to the beach, Guy. Do you remember that too?"

Blue moon in starlit sky

"Yes, every single moment. I didn't like the car ride that much until I learned to stick my head out the window, but I loved running in the sand and chasing you into the cold water."

"Those were great days, Guy."

"And so were the hot dogs you gave me from Nathan's on the boardwalk. I can still taste them. They were delicious."

"I knew you liked them even though you couldn't talk then the way we're talking now."

"Yes, dying has some advantages, but speaking of food, are you hungry, Laura?"

The rainbow bridge to paradise

"Not really, but if someone were to offer me an ice cream cone, I certainly wouldn't refuse."

Guy closed his eyes and began licking Laura's hand. Moments later a gigantic waffle cone dripping with French creamy vanilla appeared in Laura's right hand.

"That should tie you over till breakfast," he said. "I know you missed your supper."

"Even though my body is asleep in my bed back on earth, I can still taste this."

"It's the magic of dreaming," Guy explained. "It's wonderful. I dream of dog biscuits all the time and the best part is that I can eat all I want and never get fat."

Laura laughed.

"You always loved your biscuits, Guy. You were a real chow-hound."

"True, and you always had to take me for long walks so I could do my business, remember?"

"I sure do, and I still have your pooper-scooper as a reminder."

"Well, now I never have to worry about things like that since I have no body."

"Boy, I can't wait to tell everyone back home all the things I learned here. Everything is so new and interesting."

"I'm afraid most people won't believe anything you tell them. They'll just think you had a vivid dream."

"Well, I am dreaming, but it's still real."

A stairway to heaven

"For you it's real, but for them it's not. And if you tell people you talked to me, your *so called dead dog*, they'll think you're crazy. I'm sorry to have to tell you this, Laura, but unfortunately, that's the way many people on earth think."

Laura's eyes darkened and she hugged Guy tightly.

"Do even the people I love think this way?" she asked.

"Yes, I'm afraid so, even though they love you with all their heart. They just can't help it because that's how they've been taught and have always thought. Once people think a certain way it's hard for them to accept new ideas."

"That's sad," Laura said. "They miss out on lots of interesting things because of that."

"Fortunately, many people do grow and change as they get older. Having an open mind helps a lot."

Guy laid his big head on Laura's lap to comfort her, just the way he did on earth when his body was made of flesh, blood, and bone. Now even though his body was made of spirit and energy his head was just as big and comforting.

"Do you remember how you used to read to me at night from all your story books?" Guy asked as Laura petted and kissed him.

"Yes, I do remember. You always paid attention and wagged your tail a lot."

All things are connected

"That's because I enjoyed listening to your voice. Although not all of the words made sense, I understood what was happening in the story because of the way you told it."

"That's interesting."

"Sometimes people don't understand new ideas at first because they have no words to describe them, and they may have never thought about these things before, but just like me, if they listen carefully enough a light suddenly dawns and they see things in a whole new way."

"I hope that happens to me some day," Laura said. "I want to be smart just like you, Guy."

"Thank you, Laura, but I'm not really smart the way everyone thinks of as *being smart*. I'm just a bit more *tuned in* since I arrived here in the *Afterlife*."

"I think being here is like being in a gigantic library in the sky where everything you ever wanted to know is at your fingertips," Laura exclaimed. "It's great."

"You're right. In fact, let's visit my favorite place. It's called Hypatia's *Book Haven* and it's truly a paradise in print. It's named after the first woman librarian who lived in Alexandria in the fourth and fifth centuries. She was also a philosopher, mathematician, and writer. A very brilliant woman, to say the least."

Guy sprang off Laura's lap, sat up very straight, closed his eyes, and then told Laura to climb upon his back and hold on tight.

Field of flowers

Before she knew it, they were inside an enormous building made of crystal that glowed with every color of the rainbow to match every mood of one's thoughts. Ideas circled the air from shelves of open books that spoke in soft musical chimes. Each book seemed to play a different melody that merged into the whole and became a pleasing symphony. Laura had never really liked classical music before, but now hearing it come alive for the first time, she realized what she had been missing.

She felt herself swimming in a sea of electricity that connected her to Guy and all the words inside each book. She discovered to her amazement that she was able to instantly read a book just by looking at it.

"This is incredible," she said. "I'm learning so fast I may never have to go to school again."

"Isn't this wonderful, Laura. You can learn here without being taught. On earth it took me awhile to figure out how to *sit, come, lie down, and stay*. Now I can read, write, talk and think without effort."

"But I still remember the days when you were a naughty little puppy," Laura laughed. "You couldn't stop chewing on things. You really upset Mommy and Daddy when you ate the leg of their favorite kitchen chair and bit into the Complete Works of Shakespeare that you stole from the living room bookcase. You tore the heart right out of *Romeo and Juliet* and made a real mess of The *Tempest*."

GUY IN THE AFTERLIFE

Waiting for you

Guy blushed and hung his head.

"I was always ashamed of that, especially when I arrived here and my life review began. I realized I did some naughty things in my day, but I wasn't judged. I just felt lots of love, compassion and forgiveness."

"Yes, Mommy and Daddy forgave you too, the year you climbed atop the dining room table and stole the turkey on Thanksgiving Day."

"Oh, please, don't remind me."

"And what about the day you buried my favorite blanket somewhere in the backyard where I would never find it? That was pretty naughty too."

"I thought I was keeping it safe the way I buried my bones. It was how I thought back then. But you must admit none of those things compare with some of the really bad things humans do just because their thinking is confused too."

"You mean like killing and starting wars?"

"Yes, and thinking that you can do anything you want to the earth and animals because you believe they are not part of you."

"You're right. Nothing you ever did, Guy, compares to what humans have done over the centuries. I learned all about that stuff in my history and geography classes."

"All that happens because people are just not thinking clearly. I'm sure if they could spend some

The path is always there

time here, seeing how this world operates, they would go back to earth new and different people."

"When I go back, will I be a new and different person, Guy?"

"If you remember your visit here, Laura, but sometimes when you wake up from a long deep sleep, you don't remember anything that you dreamed."

"I'll remember you, Guy. I know I will."

"Then I'm happy that you won't be sad anymore wondering where I've gone. Now you know for sure that I'm fine."

"I wish I didn't have to go back."

"Well, you do, but maybe not immediately. In the meantime, there are a few more things that I would like to show you here. Are you ready?"

"Yes, I'm ready."

"Then off we go.

Paradise is a step away

They zipped along, vibrating faster and faster, as their speed increased. All around them shadowy silhouettes hovered in misty light. When Laura's eyes focused again she was standing before a long cherry wood desk where a handsome gentleman in a tweed frock coat was dipping his quill pen into an enormous ink bottle and writing feverishly into a leather-bound notebook.

"Pardon me, Monsieur Guy de Maupassant, but I would like to introduce you to my great friend from earth, Miss Laura Finneran."

Monsieur de Maupassant was at first startled, having been absorbed in a new novel he was writing entitled *Bel Ami*.

But he graciously dropped his pen and rose to his feet, extending a warm hand to Laura.

"Laura, this is the brilliant author I have been named after. I wanted you to meet him while you're here."

"I'm delighted to meet you, my charming young lady. You're just as pretty as Guy described. Prettier, in fact, than some of my French heroines. Perhaps I shall write about you one day."

"Thank you, Mr. Monsieur Guy. I too am delighted to meet you, although I haven't read any of your books since I'm only in the fourth grade, but I do want to

Let the light shine always

read your story, *The Necklace*. I know my father and mother liked it very much."

"Tell them I am most grateful, and that I was both flattered and amused when I learned that I was Guy's namesake."

"They thought your name sounded better than *Spot* or *Rover*."

"Yes, I guess that's true. *Guy de Maupassant* does have a rather interesting lyrical cadence."

"Monsieur de Maupassant's father is Gustav Flaubert," Guy explained. "I've met him too, but right now he's very busy rewriting his most famous book *Madame Bovary* since he claims he is still not completely satisfied with the ending."

"Gustav is never satisfied with his finished works," Monsieur Guy laughed. "He believes there is always more to be said and more to be perfected—an ever evolving eternal process!"

Purple field of dreams

"One of my teachers on earth is always talking about that kind of thing," Laura said. "She calls it *life everlasting.*"

"I'm afraid that has too much of a religious ring for my own tastes," Monsieur Guy said. "But then again as a life-long atheist, I was a little surprised when I woke up here."

"Me too," Guy confessed. "I think most people are."

"Well, it was very nice meeting you," Monsieur Guy de Maupassant said, kissing the tips of Laura's glowing fingers like a true Frenchman. "But now I must return to my writing. *Monsieur Georges Duvoy* is about to ask for the hand of *Madame Madeleine* in marriage, and I must think about her surprising response."

"Thank you, Mr. Guy Monsieur," Laura said with a quick curtsy. "I hope we meet again soon."

"Soon?" he smiled, fading before her eyes. "Sooner than what?"

He vanished, along with his quill pen, enormous ink bottle and long cherry wood desk.

"Wow, that was weird," Laura said, scratching her head.

"I'm glad you're here with me, Guy, or I would get very confused with all these strange new things going on."

"Well, as that nice song goes, *that's what friends are for.*"

Ruffian in Paradise

"Have you got any more surprises to show me?" Laura asked, excitedly. "I can't wait to see them if you do."

"In that case, I would like you to meet some of my new friends. I say *new,* but actually I've known them forever.

We all sprang from the same source, so I recognized them immediately once I got here. You'll probably recognize them too since you're open to that now. So climb atop my back and let's go."

They shot forward in a flash like a lightening bolt, leaving in their wake electrical sparks in the shape of stars.

Laura watched mesmerized as light dissolved into sound and sound became an opera of movement and form.

They sped through a tunnel of tall trees where birds of every shape and variety sang and danced in perfect harmony.

Riding to heaven on light waves

Then believing she had stepped into a beautiful painting, Laura gazed with awe at endless fields of multicolored flowers and long vibrant green hills and meadows dotted with gushing streams and rushing waterfalls.

"Meet my friends," Guy said, running like a new born puppy toward infinite open plains where animals of every species ever created—dogs, cats, horses, sheep, goats, lions, tigers, giraffes, elephants, pigs, zebra, to name just a few,--roamed and played together in peaceful harmony.

"As you can see, this is not a three dimensional universe," Guy explained. "A whole different physics from that on earth operates here. So there is plenty of room for everyone for all eternity."

"I know nothing about physics," Laura confessed. "We don't get to study that subject until we get to sophomore year in high school."

"I didn't know anything about it either until I held a few books on the subject from Hypatia's Library and the information just poured into my mind like water from a faucet into a pitcher."

"Boy, if I could learn that quickly, I'd be the smartest kid in class. What were some of the things you learned, Guy?"

"Well, Laura, it's hard to understand this idea, but just like *time, space* doesn't exist here either. Albert

An artist's palette

Einstein, a man you will hear about in school, wrote a whole book about this. It was called *Einstein's Theory of Relativity*. It wasn't a perfect explanation, but it did help people to think in a new and original way."

"I think I get it," Laura said proudly. "No *time* and no *space* means everyone and everything that dies can live here comfortably forever."

"Remember, Laura, language can be tricky at times. *Nothing ever dies*. It just changes form like water becoming steam, and a caterpillar turning into a beautiful butterfly."

"Or a little kid becoming a grown-up," Laura said.

A new day

"Or a dog like me who once had four legs learning to fly like a bird."

"I'm learning so many things from you, Guy, I feel like my brain is as vast as the whole universe."

"Maybe not your *brain*, Laura, which is part of your body, but certainly your *mind,* which is eternal and as vast as the universe."

A beautiful sleek black horse, whose eyes were as blue as the ocean, approached them and began to lick Laura's hand.

"Hello, Ruffian," Guy said, smiling at his friend. "This is Laura, a genuine animal lover from the earth plane."

Ruffian nuzzled between them.

"She's so beautiful," Laura said, her eyes filling with tears of joy.

"Yes, she is. Very beautiful. You would never know that when she was alive on earth she was a race horse who sadly broke her leg during the Kentucky Derby and had to be euthanized."

"I don't like to think of those days," Ruffian communicated by thought. "Although I enjoyed racing at first, it got to be boring and painful after a while, and I wanted more from life, so I decided to come here where I could live a more meaningful existence."

Guy understood perfectly what his friend was saying.

On a clear day you can see forever

"People mean well, but they still have some very backward ideas about animals. Some think it's an enjoyable sport to kill and hunt, and they proudly put animal heads on their walls to brag about their successful slaughters. Others claim they kill for food, even though it would be easier to eat vegetables, and food from nature instead of meat from living creatures."

"Well, I never liked to watch horse racing when it came on television," Laura said. "I was always afraid a horse would fall or crash into another horse and break a leg or be killed."

"There were many nice and kind people who took good care of me while I raced," Ruffian said, as she pawed the ground and playfully rubbed her nose into Laura's shoulder. "They liked me a lot and treated me well, and I am grateful for that, but other humans just thought about making money and exploiting us. That's when horses like me were hurt."

"I think some people got confused when they were taught the bible," Laura said, with a serious frown. "I know I did. For example, the *Book of Genesis* says that God gave man dominion over all living things. People thought that meant they could kill and mistreat animals. But I think *dominion* means a responsibility to care and nurture all things."

"Yes, think about it. Words can be very tricky. That's why it's safer to communicate by sending thoughts."

GUY IN THE AFTERLIFE

Blessings from heaven

"I hope people begin to wake up and think differently," Laura said, "It would be good for the whole planet."

"Unfortunately, that change won't come very easily," Ruffian replied. "Some people still believe animals have no souls and no feelings. That's why they can use us so cruelly in so many ways without guilt or empathy."

"I promise I will never do that," Laura cried. "From this moment on I promise to always love and take good care of all animals."

"You don't need to promise," Guy replied, wagging his celestial tail. You have always loved and taken good care of animals, especially me."

Ruffian nodded her head, said good-bye, and headed away to chew on some thick ethereal grass in a nearby field.

Laura gazed silently at the endless fields of animals all existing peacefully together. She saw little lambs sleeping next to tigers, and monkeys hanging from the necks of lions while schools of fish swam in clear blue waters under the curious eyes of cats and wide-winged hawks.

"As you can see everyone gets along here since there is no need to prey upon other life forms just to survive. Food is an idea that materializes and satisfies once it is willed into existence by simply saying *the word*."

Let the light shine on!

"That sounds like magic," Laura said.

"It is," Guy agreed. "And can you guess what thing gives magic its power?"

Laura thought long and hard but couldn't find the answer.

"No. I give up. Tell me."

"Love," Guy said. "Love is the magic behind everything. And you can do magic everyday of your life as long as you have love."

"Well, it's easy to love a beautiful golden retriever like you, Guy. And I love my family and friends, but it's hard to love some people who are not very nice on earth."

"I know, Laura. It's much easier for dogs to do that than people. I'm lucky I was born a golden retriever. But speaking of the earth, I think you might have to go back there now. Although there is no *time here*, there is *time there* and if you don't wake up soon, Mommy and Daddy will be very worried."

"I know, but I hate to leave here," Laura said, pouting.

"Everyone does, but until you do all the things on earth you need to do, you can't remain here."

"Will you come and visit all the time?"

"It won't be just a visit, Laura. I'll always be there with you even though sometimes you will be too distracted to see me. But just remember this—since I

Let's play

don't live in a body anymore, I can be *here, there, and everywhere* all at the same time."

"Just like magic, right?"

"Right," Guy laughed, sending her flying into the sky with the wave of his paw. "Remember I love you."

Laura landed back in her body like a bird diving head first into its secret nest. Her eyes could not focus at first since everything around her seemed to be moving and changing shape, but very slowly she recognized each object in her bedroom and eventually her old familiar world came back into focus.

GUY IN THE AFTERLIFE

It's great to feel good again

By the time she dressed and headed down the stairs to the kitchen for breakfast she was wide awake and couldn't wait to tell her parents about all the wonderful things that she had seen and experienced.

Her mother and father sat at the table talking softly when she entered the room.

"I saw Guy," she shouted. "He took me on a big trip all around the *Afterlife,* and I saw thousands of animals and dead people who were young and alive again, and then I met Guy's namesake, the author you like so much, Mr. Monsieur Guy de Maupassant and then . . . ."

Laura was talking so fast, her mother and father could barely keep up with what she was saying. It wasn't until her father took hold of her hand and sat her down at the table that Laura paused for breath.

"So you had a nice long dream about Guy," her mother said, smiling at her with sadness in her eyes. "I'm glad you managed to sleep, Laura, and not cry all night.'

"I was asleep and I was dreaming, but I know everything that happened was real because Guy explained a lot of things to me that I had never known before."

"Like what?" her father asked, sipping his coffee and watching her carefully."

"Like *time* and *space* and how they don't exist in the afterlife, and how important magic is, and how love

GUY IN THE AFTERLIFE

Yes, there are tummy rubs in heaven

makes magic work, and that Albert Einstein's book was only a beginning and not the complete truth and . . . ."

"Hold on, hold on, Laura. You're getting much too excited," her mother said, grabbing hold of her hands. People dream all the time. You must not get too crazy or excited just because you think Guy talked to you."

"But he *did*," Mama. "He *did* talk to me just as you and daddy are talking to me now. I rode on his back and we traveled through tunnels and into bright radiant lights and . . . "

Laura's mother and father glanced at one another.

GUY IN THE AFTERLIFE

Look, Laura, I can fly

"And we watched as colors became sounds and sounds became things that had shapes and motion. But one of the most interesting things I learned is that nothing ever stays the same and always strives for higher and higher levels of perfection. That's why Gustav Flaubert was never satisfied with the ending of his most famous works, *Madame Bovary.*"

Laura's mother jumped up from the table and began feeling her daughter's forehead.

"Laura, honey, you feel a little feverish to me. I think I am going to have to take your temperature. You may have to stay home from school today."

"I would never have to go to school again if I lived in the Afterlife," Laura said. "There I could just look at a book, and I would instantly know everything that was in it."

Her mother ran for the thermometer while her father sat staring at her.

"I know how much you loved Guy, Sweetheart. We all did. But there is a difference between dreams and reality, and you have to be aware of that. Some people remain confused over the difference, and they get very sick and cannot live normal lives."

"Normal lives are boring," Laura declared. "I would much rather live in the Afterlife than live a boring life here."

There is divinity in all creation

Her parents were so shocked hearing her say this, they were speechless.

"Guy warned me that you might not understand everything that happened to me even though I know you love me," Laura said sadly. "So I'm not mad at you. I know sometimes believing is hard, but I was there so I do believe."

"O.K., honey," her father whispered as he lifted her onto his lap and hugged her tightly. "We will try to understand if you try to be patient with us. You know, there's an old saying, *Rome wasn't built in a day.* Think about that Laura, and just be patient and keep the faith."

Laura hugged her father back and then jumped up, ran to her mother and kissed her lightly on the cheek.

"I love you both very much," she cried. "And Guy loves you too."

Just as Laura's parents were about to embrace her, a tennis ball that once belonged to Guy rolled noisily across the floor and landed at their feet.

Strange, you say!

Laura certainly didn't think so.

GUY IN THE AFTERLIFE

The light of the world

PATRICIA E. FLINN

It's nice to just be

GUY IN THE AFTERLIFE

Guy and old friends

PATRICIA E. FLINN

Let's play catch, Mommy

GUY IN THE AFTERLIFE

Living in the moment

PATRICIA E. FLINN

I can see earth from here

GUY IN THE AFTERLIFE

I run, therefore I am

PATRICIA E. FLINN

A day without time

GUY IN THE AFTERLIFE

Speak and I will hear you

PATRICIA E. FLINN

Transmitting thought and energy

GUY IN THE AFTERLIFE

All is ablaze!

PATRICIA E. FLINN

Remember I'll always love you!

Made in United States
North Haven, CT
17 January 2022